GRANDMA and the PIRATES

PHOEBE GILMAN

Scholastic

Toronto • Sydney • New York • London • Auckland

7 6 5 4   Printed in Hong Kong   8 9/9 0123/0

Canadian Cataloguing in Publication Data

Gilman, Phoebe, 1940-
  Grandma and the pirates

Quality paperback ed.
ISBN 0-590-74840-8

I. Title.

PS8563.154G73 1993   jC813'.54   C93-093982-4
PZ7.G54Gr 1993

In loving memory, I dedicate
this book to my Grandmas, Molly
and Jennie, and to my Great
Aunt Sadie who made
wonderful noodle pudding.

It was because of her wonderful noodle pudding that Grandma met the pirates.

On a warm summer day, when Melissa was over in the meadow picking buttercups and daisies, Oliver said to Grandma, "Ollie want a noodle."

So Grandma cooked a noodle pudding and set it on the windowsill
to cool.

A delicious noodley aroma wafted out on the warm sea breezes.

"Yum!" said Oliver.

"Yo! Ho! Yummm!" said three hungry, savage pirates who happened to be sailing past.

None of them could cook very well. For breakfast, lunch and supper they ate raw fish and barnacles. At snacktime they sucked on seaweed. When that delicious, noodley aroma reached their three savage noses, they stopped the ship, dropped the anchor and rowed ashore.

"Yo, ho! Yum, yum! We smell noodles! We want some.
Yo, ho! Yum, yum! Look out noodles, here we come!"

They swaggered up to Grandma's house and grabbed the noodle pudding.

"Unhand those noodles!" cried Grandma, but they swallowed them down,

Glup!

Glup!

Glup!

"Much better than seaweed," they said. "What else is there to eat?"

They opened Grandma's cupboard and
into their pirate sacks went:

Strawberry shortcake, mashed potatoes too,
Pickled beets, pot roast, luscious meatball stew,
Lamb chops, lollipops, peanut butter spread,
Pizza pie, popcorn, pumpernickel bread,
Cheddar cheese, cream cheese, blueberry juice,
Apricot dumplings, rich chocolate mousse,
Cold chicken salad, spicy apple strudel,
Oatmeal muffins and . . .

every last noodle!

Then, as if that wasn't savage enough, they popped Grandma and Oliver into a pirate sack too.

"Help! Help! Help! We're being kidnapped by pirates!" yelled Grandma and Oliver.

When Melissa heard their cries, she dropped her buttercups and daisies and ran back to the house as fast as she could.

It wasn't fast enough. They were gone.

Melissa looked out at the ship still anchored in the bay. She could hear the roar and clamor the pirates were making as they fought over who had the most food.

"They'll be eating all day," she said to herself. "I'll wait until dark. It will be safer to rescue Grandma and Oliver then."

By the light of the moon, she swam out to the ship and climbed aboard.

"Zzzzzzzz." The pirates were fast asleep.

How happy Melissa, Grandma and Oliver were to see each other again.

"Lower the small boat. We'll sneak away while the pirates are sleeping," whispered Melissa.

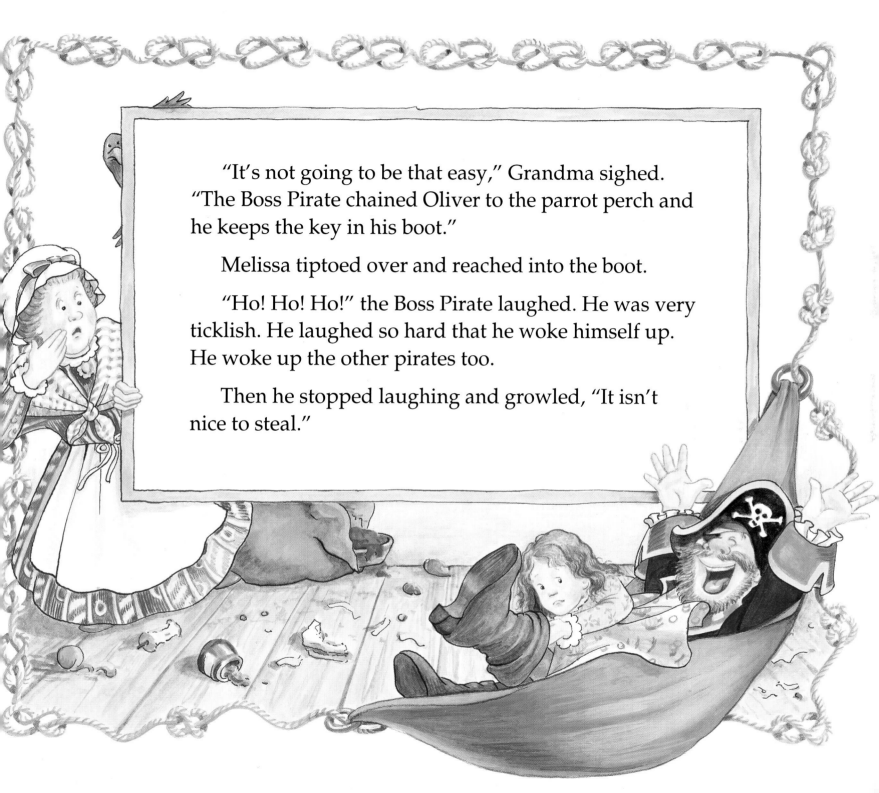

"It's not going to be that easy," Grandma sighed. "The Boss Pirate chained Oliver to the parrot perch and he keeps the key in his boot."

Melissa tiptoed over and reached into the boot.

"Ho! Ho! Ho!" the Boss Pirate laughed. He was very ticklish. He laughed so hard that he woke himself up. He woke up the other pirates too.

Then he stopped laughing and growled, "It isn't nice to steal."

"You stole my Grandma and Oliver."

"Quiet!" the Boss Pirate roared. "She's *my* Grandma now. And *you* are my new cabin boy. Start swabbin' the deck!"

The pirates pulled up the anchor and sailed away taking
Grandma, Melissa and Oliver with them.

It wasn't a bad life at first. At least they were together.
Oliver learned to sing old pirate songs.

"We are rough!
We are tough!
We are gruff, gruff, gruff!

We are gruff!
We are tough!
We are rough, rough, rough!"

Grandma cooked lots of noodle puddings and Melissa helped sail the ship.

It might have been fun, if only the pirates hadn't been so mean and nasty . . .

. . . but they were. They sailed their pirate ship around the world, robbing and plundering everywhere. And when they weren't robbing and plundering, they were teasing poor Oliver.

"He must be seasick. He looks a little green."
They'd grab his noodle and say, "Polly don't want a noodle. Polly want a cracker."

The situation was becoming desperate. Every time they tried to escape, they were caught. Once, when the pirates were busy counting their gold, Melissa lowered a boat. But the boat rattled and banged against the side of the ship.

Another time Grandma thought they should hide in a treasure chest and get carried ashore. That might have worked if only Oliver hadn't sneezed.

Then one day, as they were nearing the island of Boola Boola, Melissa said something shocking.

"We have to stop trying to get away from them."

"Never!" Grandma cried.

"You don't understand," Melissa explained. "We don't have to get away from them. We know how to sail this ship, don't we? We'll trick them into getting away from us.

"Here's my plan. I'll draw a fake map and pretend to be whispering about a lost treasure buried on Boola Boola."

23

They waited until they were sure the pirates were listening.

"Psst, psst, psst *TREASURE*. Psst, psst, psst *MAP*. Psst, psst, psst *BOOLA BOOLA*."

The Boss Pirate grabbed the map.

"Oh, please don't steal our treasure," Melissa cried.

"Ho! Ho! Ho!" the Boss Pirate laughed. "It's my treasure now."

Grandma, Melissa and Oliver watched as they scrambled up the island's rocky coast.

"They're going to love it there," Melissa said. And she pulled up the anchor and sailed away.

The pirates dug a lot of holes in Boola Boola before they noticed . . .

"Egads! Where's the ship?"